Trash Cans, Frying Pans, and a Raccoon Named Randy

Copyright © 2023 Angela Hunt
All rights reserved
First Edition

PAGE PUBLISHING
Conneaut Lake, PA

First originally published by Page Publishing 2023

ISBN 979-8-88960-457-0 (pbk)
ISBN 979-8-88960-470-9 (digital)

Printed in the United States of America

Trash Cans, Frying Pans, and a Raccoon Named Randy

Angela Hunt

Chapter 1

If it were any other Saturday, Danny would be up and running around in a cape and mask, pretending to save the world. Today, however, Danny was fast asleep under his bed with every toy gun and sword he owned. Last night, he positioned every army man around his bed at full attention and on full alert, waiting for whatever was making the noise outside to come inside. Finally, after a few more bangs and clangs but no alien invasion, Danny drifted off to sleep.

With the sun beaming through the curtains and the birds chirping loudly, Danny slowly opened his left eye, then his right, and immediately grabbed his favorite knight's sword and crept out from under the bed. He tiptoed to the window and looked out to see what he could see. Almost immediately, his mother opened the door and said, "Good morning," nearly scaring him right out of his pirate jammies.

"Jeeze, Mommy-y-y, y-you scared me," stuttered Danny, all wide-eyed and shaken.

"I'm sorry, honey, I didn't mean to, but it's time to get busy today," she said. "We still have a lot to unpack, and there is a mess outside that needs to be cleaned up. It looks like we might have a visitor at night."

A visitor, Danny thought.

In a flash, he zoomed outside to investigate the mess that his visitor made. As soon as he stepped outside, he saw pieces of packing paper, a pizza box, a few soda cans, and some other trash scattered around the trash cans outside. *Now who in the world would want to dig through the garbage in the middle of the night?* he wondered. As he cleaned up the sticky mess, he carefully examined each piece of trash until he finally found his first clue. Well, actually, his clue found him. Stuck to his flip-flop was a half-chewed, dirty napkin.

"Super D has a clue," he shouted as he held up a shredded napkin that he had used the night before to wipe up pizza sauce from the table. I think our visitor took a bite out of my napkin.

"Well," his mother said, "I am glad Super D has a clue as long as Super D picks this trash up and puts the trash cans by the road." To which he scowled and began dragging the cans to the road, making a screeching noise on the concrete driveway. "Danny," she yelled, "please don't make that noise."

Noise, Danny thought. *Ah-ha! I solved the mystery noise!* Danny pulled a lid from one of the cans and slammed it down on the driveway. *Clang!* Aha! Danny looked around to see who was watching, and then he pulled an old frying pan out of the trash and slammed it, too, on the concrete. To his delight, it, too, made a piercing *clang* on the concrete. Ah-ha! With a gigantic smile, Danny ran back to the house, yelling to his mother, "Mom! Mom! I figured it out!" Out of breath and panting, his mother fixed him a glass of juice and asked what in the world he figured out. Danny gulped down the juice and licked the pulp from his upper lip. After one big *ahhhhhh*, he explained to his mother what the noise was outside at night. "Well," he said, "I know that something digs into our trash cans at night, and I am pretty sure that either it is that stinky girl, Tallulah Vanderdonk, down the street, or it is aliens." Danny looked very convincing as he furrowed his eyebrows and scratched his chin.

When he was finished explaining to his mother, he hopped up and ran to the trash cans in the street and yelled for his mother to listen. First, he threw down a lid from a garbage can and then an old frying pan. Each time there was an awful *clang*. "See," he said, "this is the noise I heard, and I bet it is that stinky Tallulah or maybe it is aliens." Danny's mind was racing with excitement. "I will be ready for either one. I hope it is stinky Tallulah." Danny rubbed his hands together and gave his best evil grin. Danny knew instantly that he had to find the nosy trash culprit. He needed a plan and perhaps a cookie. He was pretty sure that a big, fat chocolate chip cookie would help him come up with an ingenious plan.

Chapter 2

As much as Danny wanted to be working on his plan of attack, his mom had other plans. The day was filled with unpacking; putting up and cleaning up boxes and crumpled-up newspaper; a trip to the bank; a drop off and pick up at the dry cleaners; and because he had been a good boy, a trip to the library for story hour and a book about bats. Danny loved bats. He loved everything about them— from sleeping hanging upside down to living in caves. He loved Batman, too, but only because of his cave and his really cool car. He would probably like him a little more if he was actually a bat.

Around three o'clock, there was a knock on the door that made Danny's stomach churn with nervous aggravation. With a high-pitched *yooo-hooo*, Janice Vanderdonk stuck her head into the living room and immediately began to survey the contents and goings on in the house. His mother and Mrs. Vanderdonk were coworkers, and apparently, according to Mrs. Vanderdonk, were so close that they were practically sisters. Mrs. Vanderdonk had wiry, fiery red hair that stuck out all over her head like she had been recently electrocuted and forgot to brush her hair. Danny's mother, Charlotte, had straight brown hair that would shine when the sun hit it. Janice was also quite odd-shaped compared to his mom. Janice was short and somewhat overweight, and his mom was tall and considerably smaller.

Janice didn't have to announce that her daughter, Tallulah, was with her. Tallulah made her presence very well-known everywhere she went. Danny knew what it meant if the moms were talking and Tallulah was there. Unfortunately, it meant that he had Tallulah duty. That is what he called the time he had to be involuntarily around her. It was not a pleasure by any means. She was nosy and smelled like some kind of weird spices or herbs that made Danny's nose twitch and sometimes even made him sneeze until his head filled all the way up to the top with what he called spicy snot.

The very first day they moved into their new house, Tallulah drove up on a bright-pink bicycle, ringing the little bell on the handlebars. You could hear her coming from a mile away. She didn't stop ringing that irritatingly loud little bell until Charlotte poked her head out of box in the garage out of sheer annoyance. Tallulah was tasked, by her own instruction, to welcome the new family to the neighborhood. Danny was in the kitchen with his ear glued to the doggy door and one green eye barely peeking through the crack of the door so as not to be noticed. He knew what was about to happen, and that is when his best, worst first friend was introduced into his life.

"Tallulah Vanderdonk," she said, introducing herself with one dirty, sticky hand protruding from a yellow rain slicker. "I am your neighbor three houses down and two over. My mom said that I needed to make myself useful today, so here I am being useful. I am here to welcome you to the neighborhood and let you know that the dog two streets over cannot be convinced to not chase you with even a big spoon of peanut butter."

With that, Tallulah pulled a half-chewed wooden spoon that reeked of peanut butter out of an inside pocket of her yellow slicker and put it up to Charlotte's nose so that she could see and smell the warning. "That crazy old dog chased me for two blocks while holding on to my spoon. He only let go 'cause he tripped over one of those big metal lids in the street. I was lucky to get away," she said rather matter-of-factly.

Taken back a bit, Charlotte lowered the nutty spoon from her face and took the sticky hand in hers. Charlotte was always, always, always polite. "Nice to meet you, Tallulah Vanderdonk. My name is Charlotte Littlefield." As soon as they shook hands, Tallulah pulled out a tiny notebook and a pink pencil with a cat eraser taped on it.

"So," she began as if she was conducting an interview, "do you have any pets? What about kids? Will I be in your class this year? Do you give a lot of homework? Do you make your stu… um," she interrupted her own questioning, "do you know that there is a green eyeball staring at us?"

That was the moment. Danny could feel the dread welling up inside of him come to full attention, and he took off for his bedroom without hesitation. He wasn't sticking around for this mess of a girl to butt her way into what was left of his summer vacation. He would rather have no friends in a new place than have Tallulah following him around everywhere he went. He could tell right away that she was going to be a pain and would probably want to play together at recess and eat lunch together. Heck, she would probably even want to sit with him on sack lunch day when they were allowed to eat on the playground. There was no way he was wanting to hear the dreaded "Danny and Tallulah sitting in a tree, k-i-s-s-i-n-g…" He didn't want to give his classmates any ammunition to pick on him. It was bad enough that his mom was going to be a teacher at his school. He didn't need that and Tallulah too. He would never be able to survive the playground or fourth grade for that matter.

Finding a way to escape this conversation, Charlotte said, "That was just my son, Danny." Then she called for Danny.

When Danny didn't come right down from his room, she stuck her head in the kitchen door and called again. Danny poked his head around the corner from upstairs, but he didn't dare come down to meet Tallulah. It took one more "Danny," one threat of no television for a week, and no dessert for a month before Danny dragged himself down the stairs and out to the garage. He knew he would hear about this later just by the squinted look his mom had on her face. Charlotte started to introduce the two just as Tallulah stuck out her—what Danny was sure was covered in cooties—hand. "Danny, this is our neighbor, Janice's daughter. You two are the same age." Charlotte had, what Danny thought was an evil "this will teach you not to come when called" grin on her face. "Super D, why don't you take a break and the two of you go play?" Danny's eyes pleaded with his mother to do anything else except play with this strange girl, but his mother wore her best "go play now expression," so he hung his head and managed to mumble a "Yes, ma'am" before slinking off to the backyard with this tornado of a girl. From that moment on, Danny dreaded the sheer thought of even a slight chance of a potential playdate with Tallulah Vanderdonk.

Chapter 3

Charlotte invited the Vanderdonks into the living room with her most polite smile. The best Danny could recall from every vampire comic book he had ever read, you were never supposed to invite the suspected vampire into your home. Danny felt that the same went for Vanderdonks, vampires or not, but now they are here in his home, welcomed by his mom, he was doomed. Charlotte gave him her best "go play outside" look, and as much as Danny dreaded it, he complied.

As one might suspect, there is not much that a new kid and a weirdo like Tallulah have in common. They stood in the backyard for a moment staring at the ground, rearranging the rocks with the tips of their shoes until Tallulah announced that it was boring and would just not do. "Super D is it? Well, Super D, we need to have some fun. Do you have a bike?" she asked with a giant crooked smile on her face. Danny noticed, in the sun, that she must have had a million freckles on her face, and her red hair gave the illusion that her head was on fire like Ghost Rider.

Okay, he thought, *that was kinda cool*. His mind wandered to the image of Ghost Rider for a brief moment before the snapping fingers in his face brought his attention back to the question about a bike. "Yes," Danny said as he slumped his shoulders. "It is in the garage, but my mom probably won't let me ride around a strange neighborhood by myself."

Tallulah grabbed him by the arm and said with the gusto of those stereotyped Italian women when they are trying to feed family guests, "Well, good thing you won't be by yourself then, huh? Let's go, Super D! Super D, really, is that the best name you could come up with?" she asked as they rounded the corner, opening the gate to go into the front yard and headed back inside to what sounded like two cackling hens.

"Mom, Tallulah wants to ride bikes around the neighborhood. Is that okay?" Danny pleaded with his eyes for his mom to say no, but before she had a chance to answer, Tallulah assuredly blurted out that she was very careful and obeyed all traffic rules and crosswalk signs and that every third Saturday during the school year, she was the volunteer crossing guard at Pike Park down the street. She held up her fingers like saying Scout's honor but with too many fingers.

Much to Danny's dismay and ocular begging, Charlotte shook her head and said, "Of course." Danny could actually hear his heart sink all the way to his toenails. In his mind, he heard the announcer, at the tail end of a ballgame, when he was announcing that the home team was just not going to pull out of the bag for a win. "Annnnnnd that's it, folks. It's over. They just can't come back from this one. Game over." Danny slumped his shoulders, hung his head, and let out a loud sigh of defeat. He was pretty sure in his mom's mind, she was hearing, "That's a home run, folks!" Charlotte just smiled that clever "I won" smile as Danny walked away.

Chapter 4

Danny's mind was working overtime. He could already hear the familiar taunt "Danny and Tallulah sitting in a tree, k-i-s-s-i-n-g." Before they could leave the driveway, Danny's face lit up, and he slammed on his brakes, leaving a long black kissy mark on the concrete from his bike tire. Danny threw down his bike and ran back to the house with a giant smile on his face. "Home so soon?" his mom inquired.

"Not now, Mom, I have an idea," he exclaimed as he ran through the living room and up the stairs with hurried stomps. It was only a moment later when he reappeared wearing a blue LA Dodgers baseball cap. Danny's mom didn't say a word but tried to hush a little giggle as Danny ran back down the driveway and jumped on his bike.

"Cool!" Tallulah said. "I love a good disguise." With that, she pulled a rolled-up swimmer's cap from her inside jacket pocket and yanked it over the mounds of red hair. The blue cap with pink whales on it did very little to contain the frizzy red mess. Tallulah looked ridiculous, and Danny stifled a laugh. "Got ya smiling already, Super D! We are going to have fun, I promise." They stopped a few times to walk their bikes across the streets at the crosswalks, just as she had promised his mom. Tallulah pulled off her swimmer's cap, rolled it up, and tucked it inside her pocket. "I do like my cap, but boy, it sure does get hot. I keep it with me in case I go swimming, 'cause you never know when a swimming opportunity is gonna happen," she said with raised eyebrows. "I like to be prepared, ya know."

"So what's there to do here?" asked Danny. Tallulah pressed her finger to her lip and scrunched her eyebrows tightly together, giving the appearance of deep thought, but it was short-lived. "Well," she said as she blew a tangled, frizzy red curl out of her eyes, "there's the roller rink in town, but nobody really goes there much anymore. The rink is bumpy, and the shoes stink like old gym socks. Sometimes we go down to the creek and catch tadpoles, but mostly, we just ride our bikes and go to the park." Once again, she blew a giant *poof* at the fiery tendril. Her intense blow commanded it to stay away from her eyes, but it fell down again. She poofed and poofed, and it still didn't obey. About the fifth time, she poofed so hard and glared at the stubborn mess with such fierce determination, it looked as if she was daring it to fall down into her eyes again. It took a moment, but once again, it tickled her eyelashes, settling into its home just below her left eye. This time Tallulah did not waste any time; she put her hand to her mouth, and with a mouth full of slimy slobber, she licked her hand with one giant swipe and wiped that strong-willed lock of hair out of her face. It did not fall into her eyes immediately but rather stood on end as if it was ready to take a bow for its performance. It didn't stand up for long, but you can bet it didn't fall back into her eyes; it wouldn't dare.

"I am going to show you all the coolest places." Tallulah yelled a final "follow me" and peddled ahead of Danny with her hair, like flames, kicking up from every angle. Danny had never really met anyone like her. She was like a giant ball of weird energy and excitement, but he refused to like her. He would never, could never, be her friend. He wanted a best friend, a boy, not some stinky girl who seemed to be a bit of a loony bird. He wanted a friend to catch bugs with, skip rocks, toss a baseball, and climb trees and all sorts of stuff that really only boys enjoyed. Under no circumstances was he playing with dolls or hanging frilly curtains in a fort.

They traveled down sidewalks, waving at elderly women tending to brightly colored flowers and men raking grass clippings into piles. Then without any warning, Tallulah jerked her bike from the road and down an embankment. She yelled out a bumpy howl and flung both of her legs away from the bike as she sped down the hill. Danny stopped his bike at the top and watched her as she finally reached the bottom, turning to him and yelling for him to follow. Skeptical, Danny got off his bike and began easing down the embankment. He could see the "you've got to be kidding me" look on Tallulah's face, and without thinking, he jumped on his fire-engine red bike and yelled, "Wooooohoooo," all the way to the bottom. He was not as graceful when he reached the grass-covered stump that taught him his first flying lesson. A few bumps and bruises and one really bloody elbow later, they were laughing. Danny was fine, but his mom was not going to be happy about the grass and bloodstains on his clothes.

"You will get the hang of it," Tallulah said sympathetically but still laughing.

They ditched their bikes in the wood line and started a hike through the woods to a creek that Tallulah promised was cooler than green Skittles. There is not much in the world that is cooler than green Skittles. The ground was damp, and leaves stuck to her tennis shoes. She looked like she was developing feathers the further they walked. It didn't take long to reach the creek. Danny was amazed and honestly thought that Tallulah was right, but he wouldn't dare tell her. The creek was absolutely cooler than green Skittles.

There were giant flat rocks that were scattered in and around the water. There were tiny waterfalls and gullies where the water cut through, making what Danny said looked like a slide and even stairs. Before he could say another word, a giant splash of water drenched him from behind. Tallulah was jumping in the shallow edges of the water, making her way to where Danny stood on top of a rock near the middle of the creek. She managed to slap at the water until she reached her target. The water was cold, but it felt great after the bike ride and hike, and it was welcomed. They splashed around, skipping rocks and looking for crayfish for a while, and Danny laughed and caught up with Tallulah just like they were best friends. It was too late by the time he realized he was having a good time.

Danny sat on a flat rock with his pants rolled and bare feet pawing at the cold water. "This is a really cool pl...," Danny trailed off. Looking around, he couldn't find her anywhere. After a moment, he saw her hanging by her knees, upside down from a tree limb.

"Come on, Super D, come swing with me! We can pretend to be bats!" Danny's mouth hung gaped open for almost a full thirty seconds before she did a little skin the cat and swung out of the tree. "Ta-daaaa!" she exclaimed as she nailed the landing.

"You like bats?" asked Danny, still in a little bit of shock. How is it that this yucky girl could possibly like bats?

"Oh yes," she said matter-of-factly. "I love almost anything that is upside down. You know they sleep that way, don't you?" she asked with an all-knowing look on face.

"Um, uh, yeah. I love bats! They are my favorite," Danny replied.

Danny had that weird feeling in his stomach again. He knew right then that he was in big, huge, gigantic, holy cow trouble.

How in the world was he ever going to get a best friend with her being his best "just a friend that is a girl but not his girlfriend" friend? Tallulah sat on the grass by the creek and closed her eyes and listened to the birds and frogs. Danny finally sat down beside her and inquired as to what she was doing. "I am taking it all in D," she said. "Close your eyes, and your ears will see better than your eyes ever could." Reluctantly, Danny did as he was instructed and closed his eyes. Much to his amazement, she was actually right. Danny could hear the bird in the tree that was hanging right over them, hear the water trickle over several different rocks, and could hear the frog that croaked long before Tallulah put it down the back of his shirt.

Danny jumped up and shrieked and then immediately began laughing as the frog fell to the ground and hopped back into the creek. "You are not like other girls, are you?" he asked as Tallulah picked herself up from where she fell to the ground, laughing.

"Nope, I am the extreme version is what my dad says, and I am proud of it," she said with a giant smile on her face.

Danny's mind began racing, and he wanted to tell her all about the noisy, nosy visitor that plunders through their trash at night. He chewed on his jaw and lower lip for the longest time as they sat down on the bank and watched the frog swim around and hop from rock to rock, finally disappearing in the darker murky water at the bottom of the bigger waterfall.

Finally, when he had nearly chewed off his lower lip, Danny spoke up. "Tallulah, are their monsters in the neighborhood or the house where I live?" he asked shyly, hoping that she would say absolutely not.

"Of course there are," she said. Danny waited for her to finish explaining the monsters or say anything else like "Just kidding" or "No, I am just picking," but she never uttered another word.

Just about the time he was going to ask her to explain, a steady beep chimed from her wrist. "Well," she said, "it is time to go. We have to get back home so that me and Mom can make cookies. She promised we would if I cleaned up the mess in our yard first thing this morning without a fuss."

Once again, Danny's mouth fell open. "You got a hinge problem with that mouth of yours?" she asked. Danny stuttered out that there was a mess in their yard too.

"Well," said Tallulah with one raised eyebrow, "it must be that pesky old monster again. He likes to root around in our trash for leftovers. I left him my asparagus last night, but apparently, he only wanted the stale lemon cake that had little bits of mold on it." Danny, with his wowed expression, told Tallulah all about the noise and the trash in his yard as they were hauling their bikes up the embankment. This was considerably harder but less painful than when they came down.

Once at the top of the embankment and both out of breath, they made a pact to keep the monster a secret and come up with a plan to catch the creature. They even spit on it. Danny was a little hesitant, but he was not going to be outdone by a girl, so he spit into his hand, and they shook on it, sealing the deal.

Chapter 5

Tallulah left Danny in his driveway, and he watched her pedal away all the way down the sidewalk, up the street, and around the corner until he realized what he was doing. He immediately made a yucky face, spit like every other boy would have done, and ran inside, hating that his best friend in the whole world was now Tallulah Vanderdonk. *Well, that's just great... A stinky girl,* he thought as he made his way to his room that desperately needed to be cleaned. This was not just any girl either; this was Tallulah Vanderdonk—the stinkiest, yuckiest girl in the world, and now she was his best friend. With the deepest sigh ever made by any fourth-grade boy whose life was completely destroyed by a girl, he sat on his bed and looked out the window that was partially decorated with pirate and army-man stickers. What was he going to do now? Would it really be so bad to have a girl as a best friend? *No, probably not,* he thought, *but again, this was Tallulah.*

Dinnertime was burgers and fries from the diner in town and a piece of rhubarb from Mrs. Polifax down the street. FYI, nobody should ever eat rhubarb pie. What the heck is a rhubarb anyway? Danny piddled around with army men and comics for a bit in his room before turning on the television. On channel 7, the nightly news had already started, and top story was about the nightly vandals in and around his neighborhood. Trash cans were knocked over at various homes with trash strewn all over lawns. A kindly-looking Mr. Hanly was not going to stand for it anymore. Mrs. Polifax would like to just sit and talk to them to find out what the problem is and probably try to poison them with rhubarb pie, and Mr. Thompson was just fired-up mad, and for some reason, his interview beeped a lot.

Danny immediately went into planning mode. So more than one "vandal" is going around. *Hmmmm*, he thought out loud but very quietly. "I wonder if they know that it could very well be aliens, like the ones from my comic books from the planet Toron, or maybe it was Tallul…" You could hear Danny's thoughts coming to a screeching halt when it completely dawned on him that Tallulah was no longer a viable suspect. At the same time, a light bulb popped on in his brain. Tallulah was just the person he needed to help him catch these so-called vandals.

Bedtime and all that goes with it came soon enough, but Danny was just too stinkin' excited and anxious to go to sleep. He and Tallulah—ew, that tasted gross when he said it—needed to get a trap set to catch the vandals or aliens in the act. Then it wouldn't matter if he was friends with a girl no matter who she is. He would have lots of friends because he would be a hero to the town and will have vanquished the aliens or whatever the "vandals" actually are.

The last thing Danny remembered thinking about before drifting off to sleep was that tiny piece of meat stuck in between his two back teeth. Although he wet his toothbrush, he didn't actually brush his teeth. The chalky mint flavor of the toothpaste is disgusting, and he thought skipping a night wouldn't rot all of his teeth out. Besides, some of them are still baby teeth anyway.

Clang! was his alarm clock around two in the morning. Danny shot straight up in bed, and for the briefest moment, he wasn't sure what was going on, but after a few more bumps in the night, he jumped out of bed and headed straight for the window. He was too late though. The vandals had come and gone, leaving behind the trash strewn in his driveway. The first thing he saw was Mrs. Polifax's not-quite half-eaten rhubarb pie. Apparently, aliens don't like rhubarb either.

In the distance, a dog started barking, which set off a chain reaction in the entire neighborhood. One dog would bark out some coded message, and another would respond. Then another would add their two cents worth, and then another and another and another until all of the dogs were barking all at once. Danny returned to bed, fully armed with his plastic knight sword, just in time not to be caught by his dad checking on him. Danny was as quiet as a church mouse and barely even let out a breath. His dad quietly closed his door and tiptoed down the hall, stepping on every creaking board. He heard a thump in the hallway and some grumbled words from his dad before the hall light was turned off and his parents' bedroom door shut. Another light bulb came on. Danny suddenly remembered that he had left his action figure in the hallway.

Chapter 6

The next morning, Danny was awakened by the smell of bacon and pancakes wafting up the stairs, into his room, and right up his nose. He jumped out of bed and ran down the stairs, only to come to a screeching halt in the hallway just before entering the kitchen. There was a familiar snort coming from the kitchen. Danny crept to the door and peeked inside to see his mother, father, Janice Vanderdonk, and a newspaper standing on its edges and snorting. Danny suspected that the newspaper was not snorting at all but rather it was Tallulah. He immediately turned around and began to run back to his room when he bumped into the edge of the table in the hall. The vase that sat upon the table came crashing to the floor. Danny scrunched up as tight as possible, squeezing his eyes shut, hoping that the snorts and clanking of dishes would hide the sound of the breaking vase, but that was not the case at all. Charlotte came out of the kitchen with the broom and dustpan in hand and instructed Danny to "Stop right there, mister."

"But, Mooooom," he said with a long, drawn-out *om*, "I am in my pajamas. Someone will see." He begged.

"Watch out for the glass, and go change. We have company for breakfast," Charlotte said, immediately forgiving him and almost thanking him for the quick escape from the conversation about the school supply shortage.

As Danny turned the corner to head up the stairs, he was startled by Tallulah jumping out from behind a chair, screeching out, "Argh, matey! Nice jammies, Super D!" Danny breezed past Tallulah and ran up the stairs and slammed the door behind him as he escaped to his bedroom.

A few minutes later, Danny joined everyone in the kitchen for breakfast. Tallulah was sitting at the bar counter, and the adults were at the table. A place setting was waiting for Danny with three pieces of bacon and two chocolate chip pancakes with just a dollop of whipped cream. Tallulah was hiding her face, trying not to giggle when Danny pulled up a barstool. Just as he picked up his fork, Tallulah whipped around and blew a chocolate chip out of her nostril and immediately began giggling when the chip flew from her nose and landed only two inches from the edge of Danny's plate. Danny's mouth fell open, and he turned to look at Tallulah about to speak when he noticed the bubble coming out of her nostril. They both cracked up at the same time, nearly falling off their stools. "Eat your breakfast, and don't play with your food," thundered from the table, and the laughter was cut off sharply. Both Danny and Tallulah smiled and started eating. Danny grabbed a piece of bacon and rolled it up in a pancake and stuck one end in his mouth and turned to see Tallulah had done the exact same thing. The laughter roared again, but both continued to eat their "panritto" before the adults could say another word.

After a moment, Tallulah whispered a statement that made Danny's heart race and stop both at the same time. "I got a plan to catch the monster, D! You like to camp?" Danny breathed in a deep breath and slowly turned to look at her. Tallulah just winked, and she shoved another piece of bacon into her mouth that was already full of pancakes.

When breakfast was over and the moms were elbow deep in dishes and gossip, Tallulah began to put her plan into action. She winked at Danny as if to say, "Just follow my lead."

"So, Moms, I got an idea," Tallulah said as she began to scrape breakfast plates into the trash. Danny caught on quickly and began putting juice, jam, and other condiments into the refrigerator. Charlotte squinted her eyes and smiled as she watched intently with a raised eyebrow and the slightest of suspicion. Danny grabbed up paper napkins and placed them in the garbage can, noticing that the can was getting full. He cleared his throat to get his mother's attention and bagged up the trash to take outside. Tallulah winked at Danny again and flew head-on into the plan, hoping the moms would be agreeable since they are voluntarily helping to clean the kitchen.

"Ya know, summer is nearly over, and Danny is pretty new here. I was thinking that we might…could go camping in the backyard here. Maybe we could camp tomorrow night. We don't even want a campfire or hot dogs or even smores. Well, I mean, we could make microwave smores. We are camping after all. We promise to stay in the yard and be as quiet as possible," Tallulah pleaded. In her mind, she was careful the way that she pled their case. "Stay in the yard," she had said. She didn't say "in the backyard." They would stay as quiet as possible with the words *as possible* spoken out loud but not quite as loud as the rest of the words, *but* she did say it.

With a hint of "I think this will be a bad idea" in Charlotte's tone, she agreed to allow Danny and Tallulah to camp in their backyard as long as Janice was in agreement. Janice had a pinched look on her face like she had just sucked a lemon, but she reluctantly agreed. With jeers and cheers, both Danny and Tallulah dropped what they were doing and took off to gather camping supplies.

Danny knew that tonight they were going to solve the mystery of the trash monster…the garbage alien. Whatever it was, they were going to catch it.

Tallulah was gone about an hour but returned with a wagon in tow. She had what looked like a mound of garbage bags and tools strapped down with about one hundred bungee straps. One by one, they unstrapped everything, put up a tent that would be their headquarters, and organized a game plan. "We are gonna need some bait if we are going to lure the monster to my trashcan," Danny said. With that, Tallulah pulled a pack of hotdogs out of her inside coat pocket and held them up like she had just won a trophy and ensured Danny that she was already on top of that. Charlotte and Janice peeked their heads inside the tent just to check out the progress and were a little surprised to find that a table had been erected that held tools, flashlights, hot dogs, Janice's pink Polaroid camera, and various other oddities.

"Just a minute, what is going on here?" Charlotte questioned with folded arms and that pesky raised eyebrow that Danny knew all too well.

It took a little explaining, but after about fifteen minutes of promises and "aww, Moms," Danny and Tallulah were allowed to proceed with monster hunting with specific rules that they must follow. There were pinky swears and spit-filled handshakes by both kids and both moms despite their protest.

Chapter 7

It was still a bit too early for monster hunting, but Danny and Tallulah were buzzing with excitement. "Let's go to the park and hang out for a little while," suggested Danny.

"Oh, I do some good thinking at the park," replied Tallulah. Danny and Tallulah grabbed their bicycles and journeyed down the sidewalk toward the park.

Tallulah was riding ahead of Danny when she made a sudden stop and exclaimed, "Mr. Clarence! Hey, Mr. Clarence!" Danny nearly fell off his bike but managed to steady himself just in time to see Tallulah jumping from her bike and running up the walkway to the neighbor's house.

Danny had seen the neighbor, which he now knew was Mr. Clarence, many times in his backyard. Danny's bedroom window overlooked his backyard, and he could see Mr. Clarence going in and out of his tool shed and working in his garden. One time, Danny watched Mr. Clarence pick a tomato right from the garden, rinse it with the garden hose, and eat it like an apple. It looked delicious, but he had not worked up the nerve to go over and ask to try it.

"Hey Mr. Clarence," Tallulah said, catching her breath. "Whatcha doin?" she asked as she watched him pull a shelled pecan out of what looked like a Jif peanut putter jar. "That's funny," she said, "pecans out of a peanut butter jar."

Mr. Clarence turned toward Danny and said, "So you must be the infamous Super D." Danny stuttered out a few incoherent words that brought a smile across Mr. Clarence's face.

"How did you know my nickname?" asked Danny with a somewhat bewildered look on his face.

Mr. Clarence offered Danny a pecan and said, "It's okay, son, I have a nickname too. My son, John, calls me CE. Nicknames are not bad. They are good. It is like a private, special name that someone gives just to you."

Danny smiled and took in Mr. Clarence's comment. He liked that. Before he could say anything else, hurricane Tallulah winked at Mr. Clarence, and he smiled and said, "Go ahead. They are where they always are—in the door of the fridge with the lid off. Grab a few for the road if you would like."

Tallulah ran inside, screen door slamming behind her. When she emerged, she had a sour look on her face and was stuffing something into her pocket. "Okay, Super D, you about ready to go? We have important plans to make," she asked.

Danny and Tallulah thanked Mr. Clarence with a handshake from Danny and a hug from Tallulah. "Mr. Clarence, we hate to go, but we are going monster hunting tonight, and we simply have so many plans to make." Mr. Clarence just smiled and nodded his head. Danny and Tallulah ran and jumped back on their bikes and waved goodbye as they raced down the sidewalk toward the park.

When they got to the park, they made their rounds, being sure to play on each piece of playground equipment at least twice. They spent most of their time on the monkey bars, mostly hanging upside down and pretending to be bats.

A few minutes before the streetlights popped on, they decided that it was time to head back and get ready for the night's adventure. One by one, streetlights popped on as they walked their bikes back to Danny's house and the tent awaiting them in the backyard. With excitement building, they talked about what they might see or even catch.

When they arrived at Danny's, dinner was nearly done, and they could smell hamburgers emanating from the grill. They hurried around back and threw their bikes down. The picnic table was set with mayo, mustard, ketchup, buns, chips, and sodas. After playing so hard, Danny was not at all surprised by his appetite, and Tallulah said that she was so hungry that her belly button was rubbing her spine. That girl certainly has a way with words.

"Mom," Danny asked, "do we have any pickles?"

Tallulah nearly spit out a mouthful of burger and said, "I got you!" She unzipped the side pocket of her well-worn rain slicker and pulled out a giant pickle. "I got them at Mr. Clarence's. He always lets me get a pickle or two when I visit."

Charlotte let out a little gasp and asked, "What in the world are you doing with a pickle in your pocket?"

Tallulah just shrugged and replied, "Well, you never know when you are going to be in a pickle emergency."

After dinner, Danny and Tallulah headed to the tent to prepare for the capture of the beast of Bennett Drive. The sun had already begun to set, and the frogs and crickets were singing their hearts out. Danny volunteered to set the trap, and Tallulah promised to nerf anything that dared to stand in his way.

He crept around the side of the house and then to the front, just beside the carport. Then Danny double-checked the trash cans, added a little bait, left the lid ajar, and quickly ran to the side of the house. With two heads and four eyes watching intently, the hunt was officially on. However, after about five minutes,

Danny whispered, "Tallulah, I kinda got to pee. I'll be right back." Danny, very quietly, crept around the house and into the backyard where he proceeded through the back door. He quickly went to the bathroom and headed right back outside.

Tallulah was still watching when he sneaked up behind her. "See anything yet?" Danny asked. Tallulah nearly jumped straight out of her rain slicker.

"AGH!" she screamed. "Danny, I coulda had a heart attack just now!" They both giggled, but the giggle was cut short with a little clang coming from the trash cans.

"This is it," Danny exclaimed as they ran around front, snapping pictures with the pink Polaroid camera.

"What in the world," blurted Ted.

Danny stopped in his tracks when he saw his dad with the trash can lid in his hand.

"Aw man, it's just you. We were hoping for a monster or, at the very least, an alien sent down from Mars to eat our leftovers," Danny declared.

"Sorry, kiddo, it's just me. Maybe next time." Danny's dad turned and walked back to the front door, laughing to himself and shaking his head.

"Well," Danny murmured, "we might as well go back to the tent. If there was a monster, he is long gone now."

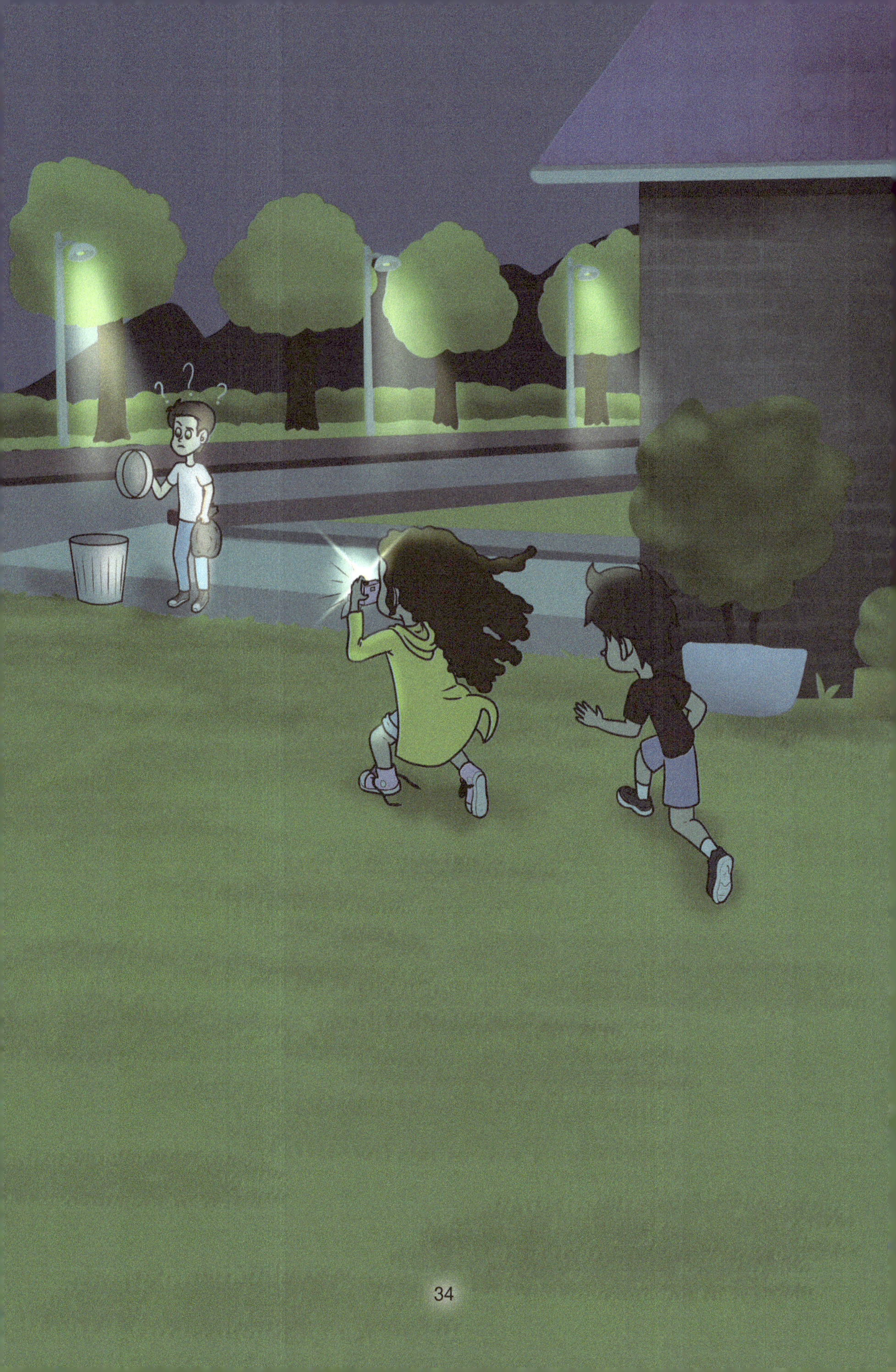

Chapter 8

For the next few hours, Danny and Tallulah played every card game they knew, including UNO, and thumb wars until their thumbs were nearly numb. Reaching into the cooler, Tallulah was disappointed to see that there was no more apple juice and grabbed the last fruit punch pouch instead.

"Can I have one of those?" asked Danny.

"Ummm, well, this is sort of the last one." Danny just shrugged and said that there were more inside. He proceeded to get on all fours and crawled out of the tent, through a maze of flowerbeds, and finally he stuck his head through the doggy door. Luckily, his dad had not gotten around to replacing the door. Danny was hoping that his reason for not getting right on it was because they might get him a dog, but his mom just said it was because he had a lot on his plate right now, but there would absolutely not be a dog in the foreseeable future.

The previous homeowners must have had a pretty big dog because Danny could fit in the door with ease. She crawled on through with Tallulah right behind him. "Don't poot," she said, "I am back here." They both giggled, and Danny immediately wished he could poot.

Once inside, they made their way to the fridge and sat on the floor, drinking a fruit punch pouch. Charlotte stuck her head in and asked if everything was okay, and they both, almost in unison, chimed, "Yes, ma'am." She smiled and returned to whatever documentary that they were watching in the living room.

When they were done, Danny, followed by his trusty sidekick, crawled toward the doggy door. Danny was just about to stick his head through the door when he was faced with two solid black marbles staring back at him. Danny froze, eyes wide and mouth gaping, then suddenly he backed straight into Tallulah's head. "Hey, I don't need a butt in my face."

All Danny could say was, "Eyes! Monster! Eyes!" Danny had seen his petrified reflection looking back at him from the monster's beady eyes.

The doggy door was swinging, but nothing actually came inside. Whatever that was that was staring back at Danny must have run away when Danny shrieked. He only saw it for a moment, but those terrifying coal-black eyes will be forever burned into his memory.

Once again Charlotte stuck her head into the kitchen and asked if everything was okay. This time Danny could not speak; the words were somehow lodged in his throat, too afraid to escape. "We are perfectly perfect, ma'am," said Tallulah with gleeful pep in her voice. "We are just going back outside."

"Well, you can use the actual door. Leave it unlocked in case you need to come back in." Charlotte let out a sigh and returned to the living room.

After a moment or so, Danny managed to pull himself together, and with Tallulah taking the lead this time, they, very quietly, slithered back through the doggy door. After a quick survey, they found everything to be safe and monster-free, so they headed for the door to the tent. It only took about three seconds to see that the monster had found their headquarters and their stash of chocolate-marshmallow fluff cookies. They had six cookies; now they had an empty Ziplock back and some crumbs. Not only did the monster devour their favorite cookies; it also knocked over a soda can that had about two swallows of flat, hot Pepsi and managed to scatter playing cards everywhere.

As they started picking up cards and random pieces of candy wrappers that they had placed into a grocery bag after eating the candy, Danny just sat down, and with a blank stare, he said, "Lou, that was certainly a monster. I mean, it was not huge, but I am never going to forget those bloodthirsty eyes as long as I live, and I am pretty sure it had fangs."

Tallulah sat down beside Danny, holding a now full grocery bag. "We will get it, Dan. Pinky promise." Tallulah stuck out a sticky pinky and Danny hooked his pinky around hers. "Let's get this trash to the can," he said.

Not really paying attention, Danny and Tallulah walked around front to the trash cans and plopped the bag into the can. As they turned around, a rustling noise caught their attention, and they both froze in their tracks. Slowly they both turned, in unison, to face the cans as a tiny furry hand grabbed the can rim from the inside. The fingers were long with little razorlike nails at each tip. Danny and Tallulah, frozen with fright, stood like wide-eyed statues and watched as a banana peel raised up from the trash inside. Letting out a breath, both took a step back and looked at each other with a puzzled expression on both of their faces. When did bananas get hands?

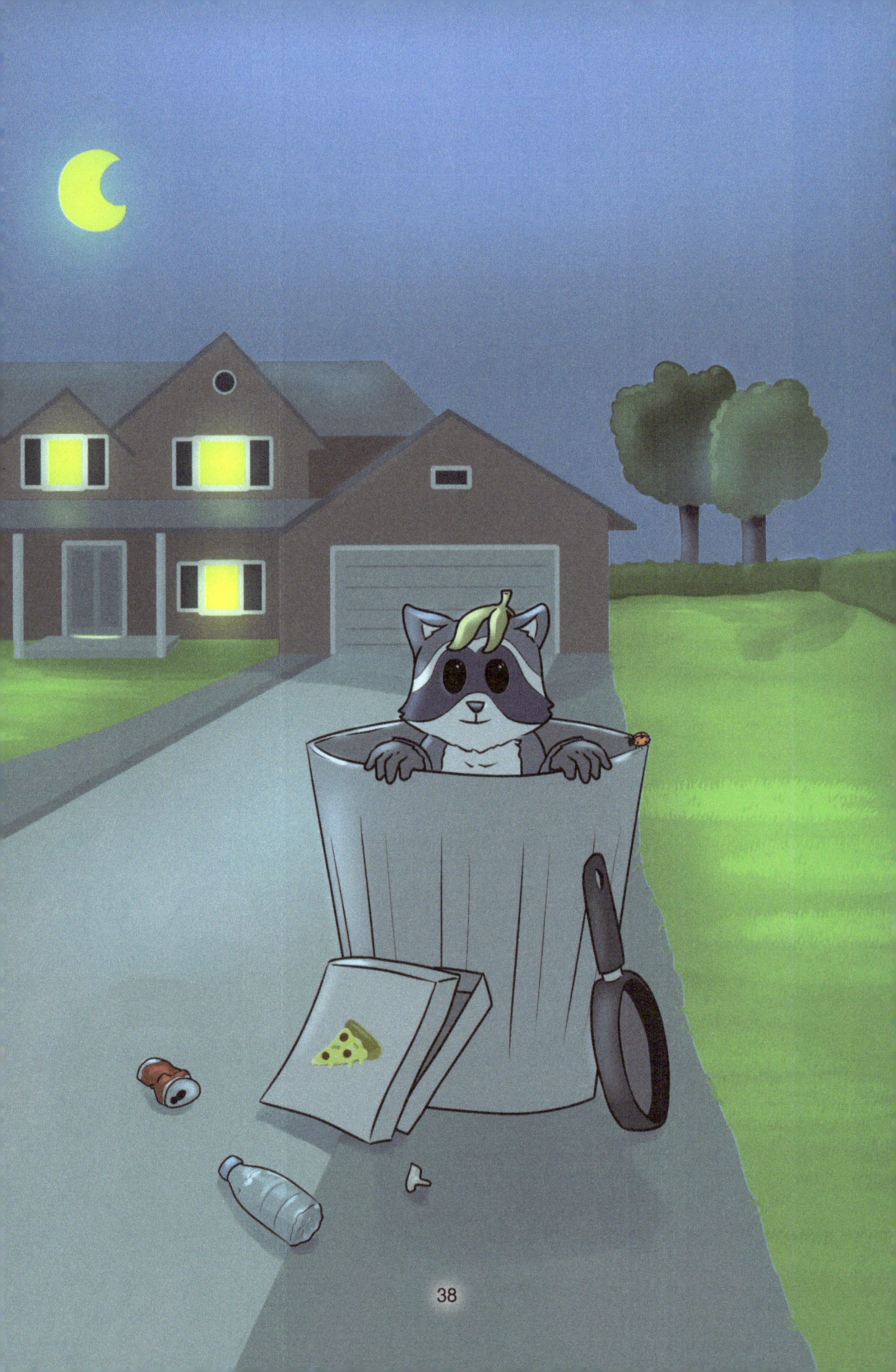

Chapter 9

With cautious steps, Danny and Tallulah eased toward the trash cans. "We come in peace," was all Danny could think of saying right in that moment. As they inched closer, a set of black marble eyes appeared and then a pointy little nose and a mouth with just the tip of a pink tongue sticking out. "Holy moly," whispered Tallulah, "it's a raccoon, and it is so cute and little. It must be a baby."

As they got even closer, they expected the raccoon to scamper away, but instead, it just raised itself a little higher and stared at both of them. Danny couldn't tell if it was frightened or just curious or both.

"Should we touch it?" asked Danny. "I mean, what if it has rabies or something?" Inching forward with his outstretched, shaking hand, Danny attempted to pet the little fellow. In his very core, he knew that this was a bad idea, so the closer he got, the tighter he squeezed his eyes shut. It was not until he felt the soft fur beneath his fingertips did he open one eye.

The raccoon still did not run away. Instead, he leaned into Danny's hand and closed his eyes. He enjoyed being petted. He nuzzled Danny's hand for a moment and then proceeded to climb from the smelly trash can onto the ground.

Tallulah and Danny both kneeled to the ground to welcome the raccoon, and the raccoon welcomed them right back. He waddled right up to them and pounced down on his behind. Danny just knew, at any moment, the little creature was going to start talking, but he just sat there staring at them both. Danny pulled a cherry Twizzler out of his pocket and handed it to him. To his amazement, a gracious, furry, little paw plucked the Twizzler out of Danny's hand and put it straight in his mouth. With half of the candy hanging out of his mouth, the raccoon sat there and waited for either of them to do something.

"Well, it looks like we have a pet," said Tallulah, "but he needs a name. Something normal, not goofy. How about Bart?"

Danny didn't need to speak; Tallulah could read his facial expression. "Okay, so maybe Bart is not the right name," she said.

Danny looked down at the not-so-ferocious little creature and just said, "Randy. His name is Randy."

A huge smile crept across Tallulah's face. "Perfect."

Randy began to waddle up to Danny, and when he reached his feet, he stood up and raised his paws like he wanted to be picked up. So without an ounce of fear, Danny picked him up. Randy scampered up to his shoulder and rested his arm on Danny's head. "Well, he appears to be a friendly alien." Danny giggled.

"What in the world are we going to do with him? We can't keep him, can we?" Danny asked.

"Well, sure we can," Tallulah replied. "Why can't we?"

Tallulah finished picking up the few pieces of trash and put the lids on both cans. The front porch light came on, and they saw the front door beginning to open. Danny quickly ran to the side of the house. Randy held on to a clump of hair and stayed on Danny's shoulder. Tallulah moved the cans a little and said, "Oh, hi, just tidying up. Some kind of creature got into the trash. You know this kind of thing happens at my house, too, but—"

Charlotte just waived her hand and said, "It's okay, I was just checking you guys." She smiled and returned inside.

Tallulah ran around the corner to find Danny, with his back against the side of the house, holding Randy. Randy was hugging onto him and had closed his eyes. "I think he was sleepy," whispered Danny.

"What if he has a family that misses him?" asked Danny with just a hint of sadness in his voice. Tallulah looked down at her shoes and kicked a small round pebble.

"You do have a good point," she said also in a sad tone, still kicking the pebble. She sat down beside Danny and ran her fingers through Randy's fur. "It is so soft," she said. Hearing them talk, Randy opened his eyes and yawned the cutest yawn in the universe. He climbed out of Danny's lap and sat down in front of both of them like he wanted to join the conversation.

Danny whipped out his cell phone and began to look up information about raccoons. "Wow," he said. "It says here that until about a year old, raccoons live with their families. Could you imagine being away from your family at only one year old?"

Tallulah squinted her eyes and stared at Randy with a tilted head for a moment and then asked, "Well, how old do you think he his?" Randy seemed to understand and looked at Danny waiting for him to reply.

"Well, I am not sure, but maybe we can call, ya know, the animal police people, and they could tell us," he replied.

They both stood up, and Randy followed suit as they began walking back around to the tent. "I guess we won't need all of our monster-capturing supplies," Danny said as they both started to giggle. Randy followed them around and played with various toys the rest of the night, but by morning, all three were sacked out in the tent when Charlotte called for them to join the family for breakfast. One by one, they each yawned and stretched. Randy wiped the sleep from his eyes, stood up, scratched his tooshie, and peeked his head outside. The sun was bright, and it was already getting warm.

The three of them exited the tent, and Randy threw up his arms, wanting Tallulah to pick him up. She just smiled and scooped him up. "Oh," she exclaimed, "he is so sweet." Just as she was squeezing him, Charlotte stepped outside and gasped when she saw what Tallulah was holding.

"Oh my goodness," she said, somewhat breathless as her hands flew to her mouth, "is that a raccoon?"

Suddenly, all wide eyes, including Randy's, were on Danny's mom. "It's okay, Mom," said Danny "he is friendly. We played with him all night. Mom, who are those animal police people? Can we call them?"

Tallulah chimed in, "We know he has a family, and we know that he is young, but we haven't seen another raccoon all night long. We caught him rummaging through the trash for food. We think he might be lost."

Charlotte stepped a little closer and reached out a nervous hand. Randy could sense that she was fearful, so he slowly leaned in toward her and lowered his head. "Did you see that?" Charlotte asked in sheer amazement. "He understood me. He knew I wanted to pet him. I wonder if he is someone's pet."

Charlotte yelled for Ted, Danny's dad, to come outside.

"What's the matter?" asked Ted. "Is that a raccoon? What in the world?" Randy just stared at all of them.

"He is friendly…almost petlike," said Charlotte.

Ted just smiled and patted Randy on the head. Danny and Tallulah looked at each other with a confused look on their faces. "Dad, this is Randy. We found him last night looking for food in our trash."

"Well," Ted said as he petted Randy under the chin, "we need to call the local wildlife office and see what we need to do with him. I will go in and make the call while you guys keep him company. There are fresh watermelon chunks in a bowl on the counter. He might like to try it for breakfast. You both are welcome to eat your breakfast outside with him this morning, but you need to wash your hands first."

Danny and Tallulah took turns washing their hands and grabbing their breakfast while Charlotte brought out the bowl of watermelon. She even threw in some grapes too. Randy stood up on the bench at the picnic table while Danny and Tallulah ate their cereal and fruit. Randy ate one piece of fruit at a time, but he had both hands full. "He really likes those grapes," Tallulah said with a snicker.

44

Chapter 10

A few minutes later, Danny's dad came out and sat with them at the table as they all watched Randy devour the watermelon pieces. They all giggled at the juice running down his fur and dripping from his cute little paws.

"I have some news," said Ted. "First, his name is actually Gigi, and he is actually a she. Gigi lives at the wildlife sanctuary just outside of town, and about a week ago, the big storm damaged the raccoon enclosure, and Gigi managed to, for lack of a better word, escape. Now, I know that you want to keep her, but we have to return her to her family."

Danny petted Gigi, and she wrapped her tiny fingers around his index finger. "It's okay, Dad, she needs to be with her family." Tallulah smiled and agreed as she, too, petted Gigi. The doorbell ringing scared everyone, including Gigi.

"Heeeellloooo," sang Janice, Tallulah's mother as she stepped through the back door to see everyone. "The door was open so I just let myself in. I hope that was okay." Janice was taken aback for a moment when she stepped outside and saw the whole family sitting at the table with a raccoon. With a horrified look on her face, she asked, "What is going on?" Ted stood up and explained in detail as he walked Janice back inside to get her a cup of coffee.

When they returned, a new face was with them. Ted cleared his throat and said, "Everyone, this is Milly McCovery. She runs the McCovery Wildlife Sanctuary, and she is here to pick up Randy, er um, I mean Gigi."

Everyone said hello, and Milly stepped closer to Gigi. When Gigi saw Milly, she hurriedly jumped down from the bench, sticky hands and all, and scampered right up to Milly, climbing her leg and resting in her arms. "Ya know," Milly said, "you have taken such good care of Gigi that I want to give you guys a reward. You all are welcome to visit the sanctuary anytime free of charge. We have so many animals there that were injured when they came to us or displaced under varying circumstances. I am sure that we could even find a little job for the kids there if they would like that."

Danny and Tallulah both jumped up and said in unison, "Yes, ma'am."

"Another small thing," Milly said, "Gigi just got a new little brother, and if is okay with you guys, we would like to call him Randy."

Again, Danny and Tallulah, with great big smiles, said, "Yes, ma'am."

As they all walked out with Milly, they said their goodbyes, and each one of them, except Janice, gave Gigi a hug and a pet. Janice was still a little frightened and kept her distance. She just said, "No, thank you," when asked if she wanted to pet Gigi.

"Oh, Mom," Tallulah said with smile, "you'll come around." Janice gave a nervous laugh and watched as Gigi was loaded into a transport crate. Milly handed Gigi her favorite stuffed toy bear and closed the crate door. Gigi settled in just fine, and with a wave from Milly, they drove away.

"I am very proud of you both," commented Charlotte.

"I am too," Ted agreed.

Looking at Janice, she smiled and said, "Well, I am proud that you both did the right thing, but could we please"—she looked down her nose then at Tallulah—"try not to bring home any more forest creatures?" Everyone roared with laughter as they turned to walk back inside.

*****

"Well, Tallulah," said Danny, "let's go on another adventure."

Ted cleared his throat and said, "After you clean up the mess in the backyard."

They just giggled, and Tallulah whispered to Danny, "I have some great ideas for adventures."

With that, she gave Danny a wink, and they stepped inside the house and closed the door.

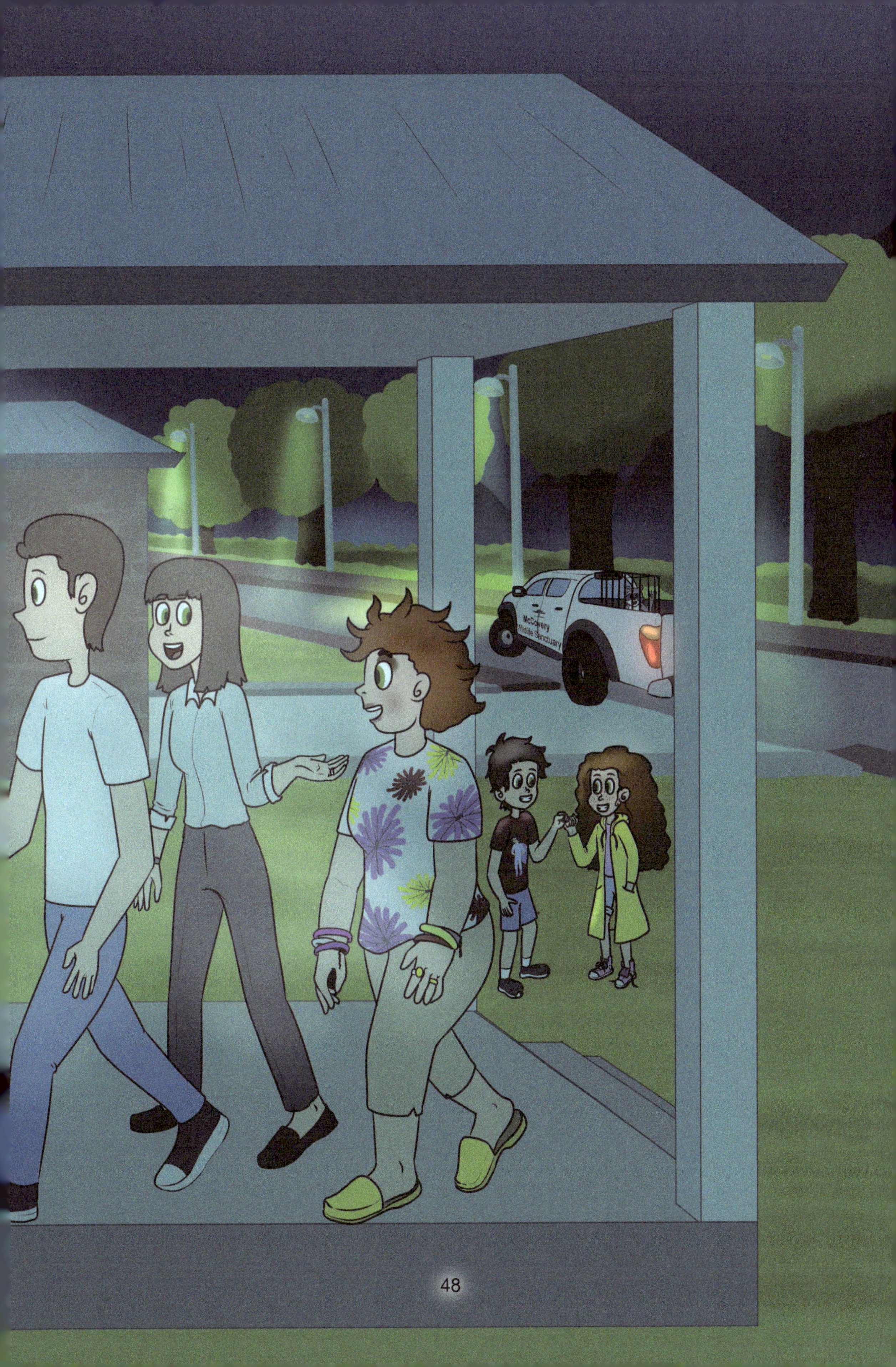
McCovery
Wildlife Sanctuary

About the Author

Angela was born in Florida, but she lived in Georgia most of her life. Growing up with older siblings, she spent a lot of time playing and entertaining herself. She fell in love with reading and eventually writing. She used writing as a coping mechanism to deal with loneliness and trauma-based events. She created friends and perfect worlds where happiness and adventure were never in short supply.

As an adult, she still finds that writing, even if it is just a few sentences about her day, brings her peace of mind. She has also found that adventure is everywhere if you take a moment to look around.